My Weird Mother

WENDY GRAHAM

ILLUSTRATED BY KEVIN BURGEMEESTRE

SUPA DOOPERS

sundance

Published by
Sundance Publishing
234 Taylor Street
Littleton, MA 01460

Copyright © text Wendy Graham
Copyright © illustrations Kevin Burgemeestre
Project commissioned and managed by
Lorraine Bambrough-Kelly, The Writer's Style
Designed by Cath Lindsey/design rescue

First published 1997 by
Addison Wesley Longman Australia Pty Limited
95 Coventry Street
South Melbourne 3205 Australia
Exclusive United States Distribution: Sundance Publishing

ISBN 0-7608-1921-1

PRINTED IN CANADA

Contents

CHAPTER 1

William's Unusual Mom

William's mother was no ordinary mother. In fact, she was decidedly unordinary. For one thing, her pet parrot, Presto, rode on her shoulder wherever she went.

None of William's friends had a mother who kept a pet parrot on her shoulder.

And to make things worse, William's mother sang. Loudly. Badly. She sang songs with lots of yodeling.

Sometimes while she sang, she twirled a rope — around and around, faster and faster, in a spinning circle!

None of William's friends had a mother who yodeled or twirled a lasso. And certainly not with a parrot on her shoulder.

William's mother did other unusual things, too. William never knew what to expect! He could see her now on their back porch, tap-dancing on the polished wood floor.

She had a special pair of glossy gold tap
shoes which she kept in a red suede box.

She'd bought William a pair, too—shiny
black with silver taps on the bottom.

She saw that he was watching as she danced.

"Come on, William," she urged, "get out your tap shoes. Come and join in! Tap dancing to music is the best fun!"

"No," said William. "I don't want to."

His mother shrugged. Then she whirled about and danced some more. Tap-tappety, tap-tappety, tap-tap-tap. And with a twist and a twirl, she went head over heels—and landed right side up!

William knew that soon she'd stop, take a bow, and thank the imaginary audience. And she did.

"All right, William," she said, puffing a little, "let's take Boris for a walk."

"Oh, no thanks, Mom, I'll stay home," William said.

It was just too embarrassing to walk with
his mother and Presto, and their old dog
Boris, in the baby carriage.

He knew his mother was delighted when
people stared in surprise at them.

But William always wished the ground
would swallow him up.

The more William thought about it, the
more he wished his mother was . . .
ordinary.

He cringed, remembering the time she had
visited him at school.

With Presto on her shoulder, dipping and nodding his head, she had played the tambourine!

Everyone clapped, including the teacher. None of William's friends had a mother who played a tambourine. Particularly not with a parrot on her shoulder!

If only she was more like other mothers, he thought. He decided to tell her, as kindly as he could. He waited until the next morning at breakfast.

CHAPTER 2

If Only Mom Was More Ordinary

"Mom," he said, "I wonder if you would act a bit more . . . normal."

William's mother stopped juggling the oranges. "Whatever do you mean?" she asked.

"Well," William said, "could you be just a bit more . . . ordinary?"

"But I am ordinary," William's mother replied, through her teeth. She was holding a cracker in her mouth for Presto to nibble.

"I mean," continued William, "I think you should be more like other mothers."

William's mother saw the look on his face, and she stopped and sat next to him. "All right, William," she said, "you tell me how to be more like other mothers, and I'll try."

William screwed up his face to think.

"Well, you see, Mom," he explained, "other mothers don't yodel, or spin lassos, or tap dance, or play a tambourine, or wheel a dog in a baby carriage, or juggle." He paused for a moment. "And if they did," he added, "they wouldn't have parrots on their shoulders."

"Whatever do ordinary mothers do then?"
his mother asked.

"I don't know exactly," admitted William,
not ever having had an ordinary mother.

He thought for a moment, then remembered his friend Kirsty's birthday party early last year. Her mother had baked a delicious homemade cake with lemon icing and whipped cream.

"Kirsty's mother sometimes bakes cakes!" he said.

"Yes, and what else?" asked his mother.

He tried to think what his friend Matthew's mother did. Oh yes! He remembered the terrific football sweater that she had knitted so he would keep warm while playing football last year. It had a big number 18 on the back.

"And Matthew's mother can knit sweaters!" he said.

William's mother gave him a kiss. "Well, I'll try to be more ordinary, William," she said. "Just for you!"

CHAPTER 3

The Hideous Green Sweater and Other Things

When William arrived home from school that afternoon, the house was strangely still. No yodeling. No tappety-tap-tap. No tambourine-banging. No chattering parrot.

He ran through the house and found his mother.

"Hello, William. Look at this!" She held up some knitting. "I'm making a sweater for you."

William looked at the sweater. It was made of hideous green, glittery wool. The stitches were crooked, and there were holes in the pattern. It was the messiest, scratchiest, worst-looking sweater he had ever seen.

She held it up against him. "What do you think?"

"Oh, great, thanks, Mom," William said as he smoothed his hand over the tangled mess.

"And guess what, William?" his mother said. "I made some cupcakes today."

William looked at the cupcakes. They were heavy and lumpy and all misshapen.

They were the driest, crumbliest, worst-looking cupcakes he had ever seen.

She offered him one. "What do you think?"

"Oh, umm, thanks, Mom." William grimaced, as he swallowed it with a gulp.

Then he looked around. "It's so quiet," he said. "Where's Presto?"

"Outside in his cage like other pet parrots," his mother replied.

Outside! But the sun wasn't even shining! Outside! Where the sharp wind made him turn his collar up on his way home from school! Outside! Presto! All alone in his cage!

William ran out to see him. Presto's head was drooped, and his feathers were ruffled.

William pushed his finger through the wire. "Presto, Presto," he called to the bird.

But Presto didn't respond.

"Presto is the Besto, yes, yes, yes," William sang to him, nodding his head.

That little ditty always made Presto bob his head, too, and in his funny, gravelly voice he'd say, "Besto, Presto, yes, yes, yes!"

But not today. He stayed hunched in the corner of the cage, feathers puffed about him.

Back in the house, William just sat. Boris lay nearby on his beanbag, looking very mournful. "Perhaps he misses his trip to the park in the carriage," thought William.

He sighed. He began to fold some paper planes. The kitchen clock ticked away. TICK-tock. TICK-tock. TICK-tock.

The house didn't feel happy anymore. Neither did William. Everything seemed wrong, somehow.

CHAPTER 4

Let's Dance!

Then it all became clear to him!
As clear as the gloss on his tap shoes! As
clear as the glitter in his new green sweater!
As clear as the beak on Presto's face!

William jumped up. "Mom!" he called. "Oh, Mom, I take back what I said! I'd like everything back the way it was."

"Whatever do you mean?" his mother asked. "Do you want me to be my old self again?"

"Yes!" William exclaimed.

"And not like other mothers who are ordinary?"

"That's right, I want everything how it was," William ordered.

"Wonderful!" exclaimed William's mother. She leaped up and tap-danced across the room in her felt slippers. "Let's celebrate!"

"How?" William asked.

"Invite your friends home after school tomorrow," she replied, "and you'll see."

The next day William hurried home, bringing Kirsty and Matthew with him.

"Is it a party?" they asked.

"Well, I'm not sure," William confessed. "At my house, you never know what to expect."

As they walked up the path, raucous rock
music came from the garage. William
opened the garage door, and the children
stood in the doorway, open-mouthed.
William's eyes widened with amazement.
His mother was perched on a stool, behind
a huge, sparkling red drum set!

But that was not the sight that amazed
William the most. There was Kirsty's
mother, playing an electric guitar!

And Matthew's mother, too, playing a portable keyboard, with a harmonica around her neck!

Boris wagged his tail to the music.

"Well, William, what do you think?" shouted his mother over the noise.

William grinned widely. His foot began to tap to the music.

Then he ran to his shoe box and put on his shiny black tap shoes.

Tap-tappety, tap-tappety, tap-tap-tap
danced William to the loud rock music.

There was a dramatic, thunderous drum-roll, and with a twist and a twirl, he whirled head over heels —

and landed right
side up!

Presto — where was Presto?

He was having the best time of all! Perched on his stand in the middle of the band — Presto was playing percussion!

ABOUT THE AUTHOR

Wendy Graham

I live near the mountains with my family, which includes two boys, Michael and James, and two dogs, a roly-poly pug and a white bull terrier — who is not much to look at but has lots of charisma! I collect grumpy-faced teddy bears and tiny dogs.

The idea for *My Weird Mother* came to me while I was practicing *tai chi* in the kitchen with my pet cockatiel on my shoulder. "Mom," said one of my sons, "why aren't you an *ordinary* mother?"

I adore chocolate, wild storms, and curling up with a good book; all three together are sheer bliss.

ABOUT THE ILLUSTRATOR

Kevin Burgemeestre

Kevin was born in Australia and has studied art and design and illustration. He works out of his own studio, which he shares with his enormous collection of car magazines and his two-year-old son, Jim, drawing, drawing, drawing . . .

Kevin illustrates books and prepares weekly collages for a magazine. When he illustrates with ink, Kevin uses a dip-in mapping pen in a loose, friendly manner. For his colored illustrations, he works in either water color with soft washes or strong color gouache applied with sponges. Kevin's collages reflect his passion for movies and cubism, and sometimes end up as sculptures.